Anne of Green Gables

Adapted by Mary Sebag-Montefiore
Illustrated by Alan Marks

Reading consultant: Alison Kelly
University of Roehampton

Edited by Lesley Sims
Designed by Caroline Spatz
Digital manipulation: Nick Wakeford
Additional design by Lucy Wain

First published in 2014 by Usborne Publishing Ltd.,
Usborne House, 83-85 Saffron Hill, London
EC1N 8RT, England.
www.usborne.com

Contents

Chapter 1

The orphan

At the station, a little girl with red hair tightly tied in two braids waited... and waited... *If no one comes, she thought, I'll climb into that cherry tree and go to sleep surrounded by white blossoms.*

Seeing a man pull up in a horse-drawn

buggy, she raced over to him. "Are you Mr. Matthew Cuthbert?" she asked, in a sweet, clear voice. "I am glad to see you. I'm Anne Shirley, that's Anne with an 'e'. The matron at the orphanage said the Cuthberts of Green Gables wanted to adopt a girl and she thought I'd do. Oh it seems wonderful I'm going to live with you. I've never had a real home before. I don't suppose you were ever an orphan in an asylum but it's worse than anything you can imagine. The people weren't bad but there's so little scope for the imagination in an orphanage."

Matthew Cuthbert looked at her in shock. *A girl?* he thought. *We asked for a boy to help around the farm. There must have been a mistake...* But he was too shy to explain, and he couldn't bear to upset the scrawny child chattering excitedly beside him, her eyes glowing.

"Hop in," was all he said, helping her into the buggy.

Anne was quiet for a while, but as they drove down a steep little hill, fringed with wild cherry trees, she gasped with joy.

"Isn't it beautiful? Look at all the cherry trees. This island is the bloomiest place. I love it already. I've always heard that Prince Edward Island was the prettiest place in the world, and I used to imagine living here but I never expected I would.

Aren't the red roads funny? I asked someone on the train what made them red but she didn't know and told me to stop asking questions, but how are you going to find out things if you don't ask questions?

And what *does* make the roads red?"

"Well now, I dunno," said Matthew.

"Well, that's one of the things to find out sometime," said Anne. "Isn't it splendid to think of all the things there are to find out? The world wouldn't be half so interesting if we knew all about everything, would it? But am I talking too much? People are always telling me I do. If you say so I'll stop. I *can* stop when I make up my mind to it, though it's difficult."

Matthew, to his surprise, was enjoying the ride. A quiet man himself, he was happy to listen to Anne's chatter, so he said, "You can talk as much as you like. I don't mind."

"Oh I'm so glad. I know you and I are going to get along together fine. I asked all about Green Gables at the orphanage and they said it has trees all around it. I just love trees. And is there a brook nearby?"

"Well now, yes there's one right below the house," said Matthew.

"Oh, I've always wanted to live near a brook! I never expected I would though. Just now I feel pretty nearly perfectly happy. I can't feel exactly perfectly happy because of my red hair. I don't mind my freckles or green eyes or skinniness because I can imagine them away but I *cannot* imagine that red hair away.  It will be my lifelong sorrow. Have you ever imagined what it must feel like to be beautiful? Which would you rather be –

amazingly beautiful, really good or dazzlingly clever?"

"Well now, I-I don't know exactly," Matthew admitted.

"Neither do I. I can never decide. But it doesn't make much real difference for it isn't likely I'll ever be any. Oh Mr. Cuthbert! Mr. Cuthbert!" she burst out.

They had rounded a corner and reached the Avenue, a stretch of road completely covered by wide-spreading apple trees. Overhead was one long canopy of snowy fragrant blossoms, and in the distance the sunset sky looked like stained glass in a cathedral. It was so beautiful, Anne fell silent for long moments.

"That was wonderful!" she said at last. "I shall call it the White Way of Delight... and isn't that pretty!" she added, as they passed a pond. "I shall call it the Lake of Shining Waters..."

"Here's Green Gables," said Matthew.

Anne saw a snug farmstead surrounded by orchards, and a babbling brook, its grassy banks sprinkled with flowers. *My home!* she thought, unable to believe it.

The yard was growing dark as they turned in, and the poplar leaves were rustling silkily.

"Listen to the trees talking in their sleep," Anne whispered. "What nice dreams they must have!"

The door opened to reveal Matthew's sister, Marilla, who stared at Anne, as shocked as Matthew had been. "Who's this?" she frowned. "Where's the boy?"

Anne burst into tears. "You don't want me because I'm not a boy? Nobody ever did want me. Oh, this is the most *tragical* thing that ever happened to me!"

A reluctant smile, rusty from disuse, mellowed Marilla's grim expression. "Well, don't cry any more. You can stay until we've sorted this out," she said. "Now, come in. Are you hungry?"

But Anne had no appetite for supper.

"I guess she's tired," suggested Matthew. "Put her to bed."

Marilla showed Anne an empty, clean bedroom with bare whitewashed walls. With a sob, Anne scrambled into her nightie and dived under the sheets.

"Good night," said Marilla, awkwardly, but not unkindly.

Anne's big eyes appeared suddenly over the bedcovers. "How can you call it a good night when you must know it's the worst I've ever had?" Then she disappeared again into invisibility.

Marilla headed downstairs. "She must go back to the orphanage and that's that," she told Matthew.

"I suppose so," said Matthew.

"*Suppose?* Don't you know it? What good would she be to us?"

"We might be some good to her," he said, unexpectedly. "She's a real interesting little thing. You should have heard her talk coming from the station. Well, I'm going to bed."

Marilla washed the dishes furiously, and went to bed herself. And up in a bare room, a lonely, friendless child cried herself to sleep.

Chapter 2

Anne loses her temper

It was broad daylight when Anne awoke. For a moment, she could not remember where she was. First came a delightful thrill, then a horrible remembrance. This was Green Gables and they didn't want her because she wasn't a boy. But the sun was shining, and outside her window was a huge cherry tree in bloom. With a bound, Anne was out of bed and opening her window.

She could see an orchard and lilac trees, a lush green field running down to the brook, silvery white birches and even a sparkling blue glimpse of the sea. It was all so beautiful she was lost in dreams, until she was startled by a hand on her shoulder.

Marilla had come in unheard.

"It's time you were dressed," she said curtly. Marilla, with no experience of children, felt uncomfortable and it made her brusque when she did not mean to be.

"Isn't everything wonderful?" Anne cried. "I'm not in the depths of despair this morning. I never can be in the morning. But I do feel sad. I've just been imagining it was really me you wanted and that I could stay. It was a comfort while it lasted."

"You'd better get dressed and come downstairs and never mind imaginings," said Marilla. "Breakfast is waiting. Be as quick as you can."

Anne was down in ten minutes, hungry for breakfast.

After they'd eaten, she offered to wash the dishes. "I can wash up pretty well," she said, "though I'm better at looking after children. What a pity you don't have any here for me to look after."

"I don't need any more problems just now," said Marilla. "I still don't know what to do with *you*. Matthew is the most ridiculous man."

"I think he's lovely," Anne broke in. "He's a kindred spirit."

"You're both odd, if that's what you mean by kindred spirits," Marilla said with a sniff. "Now, tell me a bit about yourself. And I don't want any of your imaginings. Just you stick to the bald facts."

Anne's parents had died when she was a baby. She was taken in by a Mrs. Thomas who had four other children, then went to the Hammonds where she had to look after three sets of twins.

"Were Mrs. Thomas and Mrs. Hammond good to you?" demanded Marilla.

Anne flushed scarlet, embarrassed. "They... meant to be, I'm sure..."

Marilla silently filled in the gaps of Anne's hesitant answer. What an unloved life the child had led, of poverty, drudgery and neglect. Her heart filled with pity and she made a decision.

"We'll keep her," she told Matthew later, when they were on their own. "I know you want to. But I'll have to be strict. She's had no proper upbringing."

Matthew's shy face glowed with delight. "Be kind to her. I think she's the sort you can do anything with if she loves you."

Marilla told Anne the news that afternoon. "We've decided you can stay. Try to be a good girl, and we'll try to do right by you. What's the matter now, child?"

"I'm crying," said Anne, sounding bewildered. "I don't know why because I'm happy. What shall I call you? Can I call you Aunt Marilla? That would really make me feel I belonged."

"No. I'm not your aunt."

"We could imagine you were."

"I couldn't."

"Don't you ever imagine things different from what they are? I do."

"Never," said Marilla grimly.

"Oh, Marilla... How much you miss!"

Mrs. Rachel Lynde, who lived nearby, never missed anything. She'd already heard of Anne's arrival, and now hurried up the garden path, rapping sharply on the door, eager to meet the Cuthberts' orphan.

"Well they didn't pick you for your looks," was her first comment. "And you're terrible skinny. Did anyone ever see such freckles? And hair as red as carrots!"

"I hate you!" Anne cried in a choked voice, stamping her foot. "How dare you call me skinny and ugly? You are a rude, impolite, unfeeling woman. How would you like to be told that you are fat and clumsy and probably hadn't a spark of imagination in you?" Stamp! Stamp!

"Anne! Go to your room at once," Marilla ordered. Anne, bursting into tears, rushed from the room. A slamming door above told them Anne had obeyed.

"I don't envy you bringing *that* up," said Mrs. Rachel Lynde solemnly.

Surprising herself, Marilla replied, "You really shouldn't have teased her about her looks, Rachel."

"Really!" said Rachel. "I won't come here again to be insulted, I assure you," and, with that, she swept out.

Marilla sighed and went up to see Anne who was crying bitterly into her pillow. "Anne," she began, not ungently. "Now listen to me. Rachel Lynde is my friend, my visitor, and an elderly woman, three very good reasons to treat her with respect. You shouldn't have said those things to her."

Anne sat up, her face swollen and tear-stained. "Just imagine how you would feel if someone told you to your face you were skinny and ugly. I'll *never* forgive her."

Marilla felt a twinge of sympathy, remembering an aunt's words from her own childhood... "What a pity Marilla's such a plain little thing." Even though she was past fifty, the sting hurt. Still, she was determined to bring up Anne properly. "You must remain here in your room until you apologize," she ordered.

"I'll have to stay here forever, then," said Anne mournfully. "Because I can't."

That evening, Matthew crept upstairs to see her. "Smooth it over, Anne," he begged. "It's terrible lonesome downstairs without you."

"Well, I'm not in a temper any more," said Anne, "and I'd do anything for you."

Relieved to hear Anne's change of heart, Marilla took her straight over to see Rachel the very next day.

As soon as she saw Mrs. Lynde, Anne sank to her knees and held out her hands. "Oh Mrs. Lynde, I am so extremely sorry," she declared, in a quivering voice. "I'm wicked and ungrateful. What you said was true, every word. What I said was true too, but I should never have said it."

Marilla's lips twitched. Anne sounded perfectly sincere, but the child was actually enjoying her apology. This was no punishment. Anne had turned it into a positive pleasure.

Mrs. Lynde, not being a perceptive woman, did not see this. "Of course I forgive you, child," she said. "You know, I was at school with a girl whose hair was red and when she grew up it darkened to a real handsome auburn. I wouldn't be surprised if yours did the same."

"Oh Mrs. Lynde," Anne breathed, as she stood. "You have given me hope."

"Now, run along into the garden," said Mrs. Lynde. "You can pick some lilies."

Rachel and Marilla watched Anne skip off. "She blazes up and cools down quick," Rachel observed. "That type usually turns out well. Yes, on the whole, I like her."

"No house she's in will ever be dull," Marilla conceded.

Chapter 3

A best friend... and a worst one

"Don't you like them?" Marilla asked. She had made Anne three new dresses, all alike, plain, with tight sleeves.

"I'll imagine I like them," said Anne.

"I thought you'd be grateful after your orphanage clothes," said Marilla, hurt.

"Oh, I am. But I'd be more grateful if – just one – had puffed sleeves. Puffed sleeves are so fashionable."

"They look ridiculous!" sniffed Marilla.

"I'd rather look ridiculous like everyone else than plain and sensible by myself," said Anne.

"Put one on. I need to go over to see Mrs. Barry and I thought you could meet her daughter, Diana. She's just your age."

Anne was suddenly nervous. "Oh Marilla, what if she doesn't like me?"

Marilla sniffed. "It's her mother you should worry about. If she doesn't like you, Diana hasn't a chance. Mind you behave."

They went to the Barrys by a short-cut over the brook and Mrs. Barry met them at the kitchen door. "How do you do?" she said formally.

Diana was sitting on the sofa, reading. She was a pretty girl, with her mother's black hair and eyes, rosy cheeks, and a merry expression inherited from her father.

"Diana, take Anne into the garden," said Mrs. Barry.

The garden was full of old-fashioned flowers. Anne saw a mass of peonies, roses, columbines and fragrant narcissi.

"Diana," she said, in a whisper, "do you think you might like me a little... or maybe even become my bosom friend?"

Diana laughed. She always laughed before she spoke. "I guess so," she said. "I'm awfully glad you've come to live at Green Gables. It will be jolly to have someone to play with."

When Anne and Marilla went home, Diana came with them as far as the bridge that crossed the brook, promising to see Anne the next afternoon.

"So did you find Diana a kindred spirit?" asked Marilla as they walked through the garden to Green Gables.

"Oh yes," said Anne, blissfully unaware of the slight sarcasm in Marilla's voice. "I'm the happiest girl on Prince Edward Island tonight. We're going to build a playhouse tomorrow. Diana's birthday is in February and mine is in March. Isn't that a coincidence? Doesn't she have soulful eyes? I wish I had soulful eyes. She's going to give me a picture to put in my bedroom. I wish I had something to give her."

"I just hope you don't talk Diana to death," said Marilla.

Anne didn't think she could be any happier, but when they got home, Matthew was waiting with some chocolates for her.

"I can give half to Diana!" cried Anne, heading to bed.

"I'll say this for her," said Marilla, "She isn't stingy. She's only been here three weeks but I do believe I'm glad we kept her. Now don't you be looking *I-told-you-so*, Matthew. I'm getting quite fond of her but don't you rub it in."

Anne spent a blissful summer with Diana but, on the 1st of September, she started at Avonlea school. Marilla watched her leave anxiously. She was such an odd child – and how would she keep quiet for the entire school day? But Anne came home that evening in high spirits.

"I think I'm going to like school here," she announced. "I don't think much of Mr. Phillips the master though. He spends all day curling his moustache."

"Anne Shirley!" said Marilla. "Don't ever let me hear you talk that way about your teacher again. I hope you were good."

"Indeed I was," said Anne. "It wasn't as hard as I thought. I sat by Diana and met lots of lovely girls. We had *scrumptious* fun at dinnertime. That's my new word, scrumptious..."

Three weeks later, Anne and Diana were on their way to school when Diana laughed and said, "I guess Gilbert Blythe will be in school today. He's been visiting family and only got back Saturday. He's awfully handsome but he's a terrible tease. He's clever too."

In class, Diana whispered, "That's Gilbert sitting across from you. Just look and see if you don't think he's handsome."

Anne looked. She had plenty of time, for Gilbert Blythe was absorbed in pinning the long yellow braid of Ruby Gillis, who sat in front of him, to the back of her seat. He was a tall boy with curly brown hair, hazel eyes and a teasing smile. Ruby tried to stand up and fell back into her seat with a shriek. Gilbert whisked the pin out of sight, and winked at Anne.

"He *is* handsome," she confided to Diana, "but he's very bold. It isn't good manners to wink at a strange girl."

Gilbert spent the afternoon trying to make Anne look at him again, but she was oblivious. Gilbert Blythe wasn't used to being ignored. She *should* look at him, that red-haired Shirley girl with the little pointed chin and the big eyes unlike the eyes of any other girl in Avonlea.

He reached across the aisle, held one of her long red braids, and said in a piercing whisper, "Carrots! Carrots!"

Then Anne looked with a vengeance. She did more than look. She sprang to her feet, her eyes filled with angry tears. "You mean, hateful boy," she exclaimed. "How dare you?" *Thwack!* She smashed her slate on Gilbert's head, and cracked it – slate, not head – clean across.

Avonlea school always enjoyed a scene and this was an especially enjoyable one.

"Oh!" said everyone in horrified delight.

Diana gasped, and Ruby Gillis, who was inclined to hysteria, began to cry.

"Anne Shirley, what does this mean?" asked Mr. Phillips angrily.

"It was my fault, I teased her," said Gilbert.

Mr. Phillips ignored him. "I am sorry to see a pupil of mine displaying such a temper and such vindictiveness," he said in a solemn tone. "Anne, go and stand on the platform beside the blackboard for the rest of the afternoon."

ANN SHIRLEY HAS A VERY BAD TEMPER.

With a white, set face, Anne obeyed.

Mr. Phillips wrote on the blackboard and then he read it out loud, so that even the youngest pupils who couldn't yet read should understand it.

Anne stood there for the rest of the afternoon. She did not cry. She was too angry for that, and when school was dismissed, she marched out, her head held high.

"I'm awful sorry I made fun of your hair," Gilbert whispered. "Please don't be mad for keeps."

Anne simply swept past him, as if he were not there.

"How could you ignore him?" breathed Diana. "I don't think I could."

"I shall never forgive Gilbert Blythe,"

said Anne, firmly. "And Mr. Phillips spelled my name without an 'e' too. The iron has entered my soul, Diana," she declared.

Diana hadn't the least idea what Anne meant but she understood it was something terrible.

"You mustn't mind Gilbert," she said, soothingly. "He makes fun of all us girls. He calls me crow all the time because of my black hair. And I never heard him apologize for anything before."

"There's a great deal of difference being called a crow and being called carrots," said Anne with dignity. "Gilbert Blythe has hurt my feelings *excruciatingly*."

From then on, whenever she saw Gilbert, Anne passed him with an icy contempt, despite his obvious desire to be friends. Even Diana's attempts at peacemaking were to no avail. Anne had made up her mind to hate Gilbert Blythe for the rest of their lives.

Chapter 4

The disastrous tea party

At school, Anne worked even harder now to beat Gilbert Blythe. October came and the wild cherry trees and maples turned crimson and bronzy green.

"Oh Marilla," Anne exclaimed, dancing in one Saturday morning, her arms filled with gorgeous boughs. "I'm so glad I live in a world where there are Octobers. It would be terrible if we just skipped from September to November, wouldn't it? I'm going to decorate my room with these maple branches."

"Such clutter," scolded Marilla. "Bedrooms are for sleeping..."

"And for dreaming..."

Marilla sighed. "Well, mind you don't drop leaves all over the stairs. Now," she went on, "I'm going out this afternoon and won't be home before dark so you'll have to get Matthew his supper. And, I don't know if I'm doing right; you're such a flibbertigibbet girl, but you can ask Diana to spend the afternoon and stay for tea."

"Marilla, how lovely!" Anne cried. "You *are* able to imagine things. How else did you know I longed to have a guest? It will feel so grown-uppish."

"You may cut some fruitcake and have some cookies," said Marilla. "And there's a bottle half-full of raspberry cordial on the second shelf of the pantry, if you'd like that to drink."

Anne flew off to ask Diana to tea, with the result that, just after Marilla drove off,

Diana arrived dressed in her second-best dress and knocked at the front door.

Anne answered it, wearing *her* second best, and both girls shook hands as if they had never met before.

"How is your mother?" she asked, after they had sat for ten minutes in unnatural silence in the sitting room.

"Very well, thank you," Diana replied. "The crops are good this year," she added. "Have you picked your apples yet?"

"Oh, ever so many," said Anne, forgetting to be dignified. "Let's go to the orchard and pick some now."

The orchard was so delightful, they spent most of the afternoon sitting in the warm sunshine, eating apples and talking.

But when Diana mentioned Gilbert Blythe, Anne jumped up. "Time for tea!" she declared.

She looked everywhere for the cordial, finally finding it tucked away on the top shelf. Anne put it on a tray with a tumbler and set it before Diana.

"Now please help yourself," she said politely. "I don't think I can manage any just now after all those apples."

Diana poured herself a tumblerful, admiring its bright red hue before sipping it daintily. "That's awfully nice raspberry cordial, Anne," she said. "I didn't know raspberry cordial was so nice."

"I'm glad you like it," said Anne. "Take as much as you want."

So Diana gulped down a second and then a third. The tumblerfuls were generous and the cordial was delicious.

"The nicest I ever drank," said Diana. "Much nicer than Mrs. Lynde's. It doesn't taste a bit like hers."

"I should think Marilla's would be much nicer," Anne said loyally. "She's a famous cook. She's trying to teach me but it's so hard. There's so little scope for imagination in cookery. The last time I made a cake I was imagining the loveliest story. I forgot the flour and the cake was a dismal failure. Flour is essential to cakes, you know. Why, Diana, what *is* the matter?"

Diana had stood up unsteadily, and sat down again, putting her hands to her head. "I'm-I'm awful sick," she said. "I must go home."

"You can't go without tea!" cried Anne.

"I must go home," Diana repeated. "I feel dizzy."

And indeed she walked dizzily.

Anne helped walk her to the Barry house and then she wept all the way back to Green Gables.

The next day, Anne went on an errand to Mrs. Lynde's and returned in no time, sobbing uncontrollably.

"Marilla," she wailed, "Mrs. Lynde met Mrs. Barry who said I deliberately made Diana drunk. I only gave her raspberry cordial. I didn't think cordial could make people drunk even if they drank three big tumblerfuls."

"Drunk fiddlesticks!" said Marilla, marching to the pantry. There on the shelf she saw a bottle of her homemade wine. "Anne! You gave Diana currant wine instead of raspberry cordial. Now I think of it, I put the cordial in the cellar. But couldn't you tell the difference?"

"I've never tasted either," Anne said. "And Mrs. Barry is so angry. She'll never believe I didn't do it on purpose."

"There, child, don't cry. It's not your fault. We'll go to see her and explain."

But Mrs. Barry refused to listen to either of them. Coldly, she informed Anne, "You won't play with Diana ever again."

At that, Marilla lost her temper. "If I had a child who was so greedy as to drink three glasses of anything, I'd sober her up with a right good spanking."

As they left, Diana was in the garden, crying. "Goodbye, Anne. I'll never love another friend like you."

Anne drew a deep breath. "You love me? Nobody has ever loved me for as long as I can remember. Oh, this is wonderful! You've cast a ray of light on today's darkness. Goodbye, my dearest friend."

Anne waved until Diana was out of sight. Then she turned to Marilla and announced solemnly, "It is all over. I shall never have another friend. My farewell to Diana will be sacred in my memory forever. I don't believe I'll live very long now. I'll die of grief. Perhaps when she sees me lying cold and dead before her, Mrs. Barry will be sorry, and let Diana come to my funeral."

"I don't think you're dying," said Marilla unsympathetically. "You talk too much!"

Chapter 5

Anne to the rescue

All winter, Diana was forbidden even to talk to Anne at school. Then, one evening, while Marilla was away, the kitchen door was flung open and Diana rushed in, white-faced and breathless.

"Oh Anne, do come quick," implored Diana. "My little sister, Minnie May, is sick with croup and Mother and Father are out and I don't know what to do."

Matthew silently took his coat and cap and slipped past Diana into the yard.

"He's gone to harness the mare and get the doctor," said Anne, as she flung on her coat and hood. "I know it as if he'd said so. Don't worry, Di, I've nursed three sets of twins with croup. Marilla has the right medicine here."

The two girls hurried across snow encrusted fields. The night was clear and frosty, all ebony and silver, with big stars shining over silent fields and, here and there, dark pointed firs, their branches powdered with snow.

Anne, though truly sorry for Minnie May, thrilled to the romance of racing through the mysterious night with the best friend she hadn't spoken to for so long.

Minnie May, aged three, was very sick. She lay on the kitchen sofa, feverish and restless, and her hoarse breathing could be heard all over the house.

Anne put her to bed, measured out the medicine and dosed her through the night.

It was three o'clock in the morning when Matthew arrived with a doctor, having ridden several towns away to find one. By then, Minnie May was much better and sleeping soundly.

"That little red-headed girl saved her life," the doctor told Mrs. Barry later.

Anne went home with Matthew through the white-frosted morning, heavy-eyed from lack of sleep but still talking.

"Isn't it a wonderful morning? I'm so glad I live in a world with white frosts. And I'm glad Mrs. Hammond had three sets of twins or I mightn't have known what to do. But I'm so sleepy..."

"You just go right to bed," advised

Matthew, looking at Anne's white, tired face. "Have a good sleep."

Anne slept so long and so soundly, it was well into the rosy winter afternoon when she awoke and went down to the kitchen.

Marilla, who had returned earlier that afternoon, looked up from her knitting. "Your dinner is in the oven. I guess you're hungry. Matthew told me about last night. I must say it was fortunate you knew what to do. There now, never mind talking till you've eaten. I can tell you're just full up with speeches but they'll keep."

Marilla had some news but knew Anne would be too excited to eat if she heard it just then. Not until Anne had finished a plate of blue plums did Marilla say:

"Mrs. Barry was here this afternoon Anne, but I wouldn't wake you up. She says you saved Minnie May's life and she's very sorry she acted as she did. She knows now you didn't mean to get Diana drunk.

She hopes you'll forgive her and be friends with Diana again. You can go now but – Anne Shirley, are you crazy? Come back this instant for a coat!"

But Anne was already gone.

She came dancing home in the purple winter twilight. Sleigh bells rang out among the snowy hills but their music was not as sweet as the song in Anne's heart.

"You see before you a perfectly happy person, Marilla," she announced. "Yes, in spite of my red hair. Mrs. Barry kissed me and cried and said she could never repay me. I was dreadfully embarrassed but I just said, 'I have no hard feelings. Henceforth I shall cover the past with the mantle of oblivion.' And then we had tea."

"You've done well," said Marilla.

Chapter 6

A concert and puffed sleeves

"Dear me, there is nothing but meetings and partings in this world, as Mrs. Lynde would say," Anne remarked as she came in from school one afternoon, wiping her eyes with a damp handkerchief.

"I didn't think you were that fond of your teacher," said Marilla.

"I don't think I cried because Mr. Phillips was leaving," said Anne. "I cried because all the other girls did. And he made such a beautiful speech beginning, 'The time has come for us to part.' We cried all the way home, but then we met the new minister and his wife. She had such a lovely dress with puffed sleeves.

How I long for puffed sleeves... But I've heard such exciting things about our new teacher. Her name is Miss Stacy and she's perfectly sweet."

To Anne's delight, Miss Stacy wore the biggest puffed sleeves in Avonlea and turned out to be another kindred spirit.

As the months passed, Anne blossomed and came home with glowing accounts of school. "I love Miss Stacy with my whole heart, Marilla. When she says my name I feel *instinctively* that she's spelling it with an 'e'. And she's organizing a concert for us all to be in on Christmas night!"

"She's filling your head with foolish nonsense," grumbled Marilla. "I don't hold with children getting up concerts when they should be at their lessons."

Still, Anne threw herself into the concert heart and soul, and even Marilla's disapproval couldn't stop her.

"I'll be heartily glad when it's all over,"

was all Marilla had to say, so Anne went to find Matthew, sure of an appreciative and sympathetic listener.

"I'm reciting two pieces and I tremble when I think of it, but it's a nice thrilly kind of tremble."

"Well now, I reckon it's going to be a pretty good concert. And I expect you'll do your part fine," he said, smiling into her eager little face.

Anne smiled back and Matthew thanked his stars he had nothing to do with bringing her up. It left him free to 'spoil Anne' (in Marilla's words) as much as he liked.

Several days later, he went into the kitchen, unaware that Anne and her schoolfriends were rehearsing in the sitting room. Presently they came trooping through, laughing and chattering, not noticing Matthew who shrank shyly into the shadows.

He watched in silence as they put on caps and jackets and talked about the concert. Anne stood among them, bright-eyed and animated, but there was something different about her, something not quite right. What was it?

Matthew was haunted by the question long after Anne's friends had left and she had taken herself off with her books. He couldn't ask Marilla, who, he felt sure, would sniff scornfully and remark that the only difference between Anne and the other girls, was that the other girls were sometimes quiet.

After two hours, he came up with the answer: Anne wasn't dressed like the other girls! Marilla kept her clothed in plain, dark dresses. But surely it would do no harm for her to have one pretty dress – and Christmas was only a fortnight off. A new dress would be the very thing...

"Oh Matthew! Is that for me?" Anne breathed as he held out the dress on Christmas morning. She took it and looked at it in silence. How pretty it was, in glossy silk with frills and ruffles, but the sleeves were the crowning glory with two beautiful puffs above the elbows.

"Anne?" said Matthew, shyly, "Don't you like it?"

Anne's eyes filled with tears. "Like it? It's exquisite. I can never thank you enough."

"It's for my girl," said Matthew. "My girl that I'm proud of."

He was even prouder when Anne performed in the concert wearing her new dress and with tiny roses in her hair.

"I was so nervous," she confessed to Diana, once it was all over. "But I thought of my puffed sleeves and they gave me courage."

"You were lovely," Diana assured her. "And wait till I tell you. One of the roses fell out of your hair and Gilbert Blythe picked it up and put it in his pocket!"

"It's nothing to me what he does," Anne replied loftily.

"I was real proud of Anne this evening," Matthew told Marilla that night.

"I was too," admitted Marilla, "but I wouldn't dream of telling her so."

Chapter 7

Vanity and vexation

One April evening, heading back from a meeting, Marilla thought with satisfaction that Anne had improved in every way. There was sure to be a briskly crackling fire in the kitchen, the table laid for tea, a freshly baked cake waiting...

Nothing had been done. The house was dark and silent.

"Anne!" Marilla called. "Where are you?" Eventually she found Anne in bed, face down in the pillows. "Are you sick?"

"No... Please go away and don't look at me. I'm in the depths of despair."

"Why?"

"I've got green hair," faltered Anne.

"I dyed it."

Marilla, peering in candlelight, saw grotesque green streaks with the original red showing through.

"I thought nothing could be as bad as red hair," moaned Anne. "I was wrong. Green is worse."

"Why dye it *green*, for goodness sake?"

"I bought the dye from a man who came to the door. He swore my hair would turn a beautiful raven black and wouldn't wash off. Oh, what shall I do?"

"Well the first thing is to give your hair a good washing."

Anne scrubbed it vigorously but it made no difference. In that, at least, the man had told the truth.

"I can't go to school," she wailed. "How Josie Pye will laugh. Marilla, I *cannot* face Josie Pye."

"It's no use, Anne," said Marilla. "Your hair must be cut off."

Anne's clipped head made a sensation in school the next day, but to her relief nobody guessed the real reason for it, though Josie told her she looked a perfect scarecrow.

"Josie is a Pye," said Marilla, "so she can't help being disagreeable. I suppose people like that must serve some useful purpose in society, but I'm sure I don't know what it is, any more than I know the use of thistles."

"I didn't say anything," said Anne, "just swept her one scornful look and then forgave her. It makes you feel very virtuous when you forgive people. I mean to concentrate on being good after this. I shall never try to be beautiful again."

Anne didn't try, but to her delight, her hair grew back much darker. "Do you think it could be called auburn?" she asked Diana one day, when they were playing by the pond near the Barrys' house.

"Yes, and it's really pretty," said Diana.

They were acting out a poem by Tennyson and Anne was sent floating across the pond on a boat, pretending to be dead.

For a few moments, she enjoyed the romance of the situation, but then her boat began to leak. It rapidly started to

sink but, just as Anne thought all hope was lost, Gilbert Blythe came rowing past.

"Anne Shirley! What happened?" he exclaimed, pulling close to her and holding out a hand to help her onto his boat.

"I was a maiden in a poem," said Anne coldly, not even looking at him. "Would you be so kind as to take me to the bank?"

They rowed over in silence and Anne sprang nimbly ashore. "I'm very much obliged to you," she said haughtily, as she turned away.

Gilbert leaped from the boat and laid a hand on her arm. "Anne," he said. "I'm awfully sorry I made fun of your hair. I think it's really pretty. Let's be friends."

Anne hesitated, her heart giving a quick, queer little beat. But then the old bitterness and resentment rose up. "No," she said as coldly as before. "I shall never be friends with you, Gilbert Blythe!"

"All right!" Gilbert sprang back into his

boat, his cheeks flushed an angry red. "I'll never ask you again, Anne Shirley."

Anne wished suddenly she'd replied differently. But it was too late.

"Will you *ever* have any sense, Anne?" groaned Marilla, when she heard about the sinking boat.

"Oh yes," replied Anne. "I think my prospects of becoming sensible are brighter than ever. I've realized it's no good trying to be romantic in Avonlea. Nearly drowning has cured me of fanciful ideas and romance."

"I hope so," said Marilla.

But Matthew laid a hand on Anne's shoulder. "Don't give up on all your romance," he whispered shyly. "A little romance is a good thing. Keep a little of it, Anne, keep a little."

Chapter 8

Love, loss and friendship

Anne did keep some romance, though she became quieter as she grew up and began to make plans for college. She was coming into the kitchen one day, her arms full of flowers, when she heard Marilla cry, "Matthew! What's the matter?"

Matthew stood in the doorway, his face strangely drawn. Then, without a word, he collapsed.

"He's fainted," said Marilla.

"Oh, Marilla... you don't think he's... he can't be..." Anne could not say the dreadful word, but it was true. Matthew had suffered a heart attack and could not be revived.

That night, unable to sleep, she heard in her head Matthew's voice repeating, *My girl that I'm proud of...*

"What will we do without him?" she sobbed out loud, until Marilla came.

"We have each other," comforted Marilla. "It's never been easy for me to say what I feel, but I tell you, I love you as dearly as if you were my own flesh and blood, and you've been my joy and comfort ever since you came to Green Gables."

"Oh Marilla, keep your arm around me."

Every day, after the funeral, Anne laid flowers on Matthew's grave. One evening, she walked on in the sunset to the Lake of Shining Waters.

There she saw Gilbert, who lifted his cap courteously. He would have passed on in silence if Anne had not held out her hand.

"Gilbert," she said, with scarlet cheeks. "I'm sorry I've kept up our feud for so long.

What a stubborn little goose I was. I've been sorry since that day by the pond."

Gilbert held her hand. "We're going to be the best of friends from now on," he said jubilantly. "We were born to be good friends, Anne. Come, I'll walk you home."

And they headed off to Green Gables, with years of conversations to catch up on. The wind whispered in the cherry boughs and stars twinkled above the firs.

"Isn't the world lovely," Anne murmured. "I am glad to be in it."

The pain of losing Matthew was still sharp, but she had Marilla, and Diana, and now Gilbert too. Who knew what the next few years would bring?

Lucy Maud Montgomery
(1874-1942)

Lucy Maud Montgomery, known as Maud, was born on Prince Edward Island on the east coast of Canada.

Her mother died when she was only 21 months old, and she was brought up by her grandparents. Maud's early life was lonely, so she turned to books and writing, creating dozens of imaginary friends. These not only kept her company, they stretched her imagination and fired her creativity.

Her first poem was published when she was just 16. After leaving school, she was briefly a teacher, but all the while she was writing – it was her passion and a way to escape the world.

Anne of Green Gables was Maud's first novel. Published in 1908, it was an immediate hit. Though she wrote many other books, including several sequels to the *Anne* books, *Anne of Green Gables* remains the most famous.